Sorry, I can't play right now.
I'm getting ready to run away from home.
And you know what that's like, right?

What's that? You've never run away?
Okay, then, stick around. I'll show you how it's done.

If you're planning to run away, the first thing you need is a reason.

Like maybe your parents are going gaga over your little sister and ignoring you. So what if she's a baby? You were here first.

Not fair!

Or maybe your brother gets to stay up a whole hour later even though he's a big warty slug. Your mom says it's because he's older. But you know it's because she likes him better.

Or it might be that your mother threw away your *entire* collection of candy wrappers that you'd been saving forever and planned to wallpaper your bedroom with.

If you're not sure your reason's good enough, try it out loud.

I'M RUNNING AWAY AND NEVER COMING BACK BECAUSE YOU THREW OUT ALL MY CANDY WRAPPERS AND RUINED MY WHOLE LIFE!

Did it sound okay? Keep practicing until it does.

Now you have to pack.

Forget about tying a bandana to a stick. You'll need something way bigger. A backpack, at least. Or better yet, a wagon. Because remember: You're never *ever* coming home.

You'll also need snacks: graham crackers and gummy worms and packets of hot chocolate. Oh, and gum. So you don't need a toothbrush.

You're too grown-up for a stuffed animal, but take your favorite one anyway. That will show your parents you mean business.

And you'll need a pillow and a blanket. But no pajamas. Out on your own, you get to sleep in your clothes.

Save room for a bow and arrow. In case there are bears.

Time to say goodbye to your pets. Bury your face in their fur and tell them how sorry you are to leave them. It's not their fault your family's so mean. (You can just wave at the fish.)

If there's room in your wagon, pick one pet to take along. Hint: Choose one that won't eat your snacks.

And now for the most important part.
Write a note.

Why I ran away
(like anyone cares)
It's never my turn to
pick the TY show.
That dumb baby.
Not allowed to keep
pet squirrel. Have
to wear sweater vests
to Grandma's.
Peas. PEAS.
PEAS.

Imagine your parents' faces when they
read it. If they look like they're about to burst
into tears, you'll know your note is perfect.

Tape the note where
your parents can't miss it.

Now comes the big moment. . . .

You're ready to storm out of the house!
Stomp your feet and make lots of noise.
Then holler that line you practiced earlier.
See if you can work in a little sob.

Once you're outside, decide where you're going. Your best friend's house? His big sister gets to stay up late, too, so he'll know just how you feel.

Or how about Grandma's house? She still likes you, even if you're not as cute as the baby.

Or maybe the park. There's a slide and tire
swings and enough other kids to keep you busy
all day. And when everyone goes home, you can
hide behind a trash can.

At night you can sleep on a bench. Thank goodness
for your blanket and pillow!

Wherever you're headed, DO NOT LOOK BACK.

Do not—I repeat, do NOT—think about how your dad taught you to swim.

Or the time your brother helped you find rocks for your collection.

Or your mom's spaghetti.

Or how silly your baby sister looks when she laughs.

Or how cozy it is in your nice warm bed.

When you can't see your house anymore, stop for a snack. But don't dawdle, because your folks might come looking for you. And you don't want them to find you. Because they're the worst family in the world.

Here's where things get tricky. The truth is, they probably won't come looking. Even if you sit on the sidewalk and wait in broad daylight.

So you need to decide. Do you really want to stay at your best friend's and go to bed before his sister? Might as well be home. Maybe Grandma's house isn't such a great idea, either. She might put you to work.

And suddenly sleeping in the park doesn't sound that exciting. I mean, what if there really was a bear?

Maybe you'll give your folks one last chance—
even though they don't deserve it.

Once you're home, things might not seem as bad as you remembered. You can always collect more candy wrappers, right?

But don't let your family know you feel that way.

Because they'd better
start treating you right.
And if they don't . . .

. . . you might just run away
from home again.

For Sophie Jane and Charles Kane.
I'm glad you both came home. —J.L.H.

To my mother, who never ran away —R.N.S.

Text copyright © 2013 by Jennifer LaRue Huget
Jacket and interior illustrations copyright © 2013 by Red Nose Studio
All rights reserved. Published in the United States by
Schwartz & Wade Books, an imprint of Random House Children's Books,
a division of Random House, Inc., New York.

Schwartz & Wade Books and the colophon are trademarks of Random House, Inc.

Visit us on the Web! randomhouse.com/kids

Educators and librarians, for a variety of teaching tools, visit us at
RHTeachersLibrarians.com

Library of Congress Cataloging-in-Publication Data
Huget, Jennifer LaRue.
The beginner's guide to running away from home / Jennifer LaRue Huget ; illustrated by Red Nose Studio.
1st ed.   p. cm.
Summary: A child provides unique advice on how to run away from home—and come back.
ISBN 978-0-375-86739-2 (trade : alk. paper) — ISBN 978-0-375-96739-9 (glb : alk. paper)
[1. Family life—Fiction. 2. Humorous stories.] I. Red Nose Studio. II. Title.
PZ7.H872958 Beg 2013   [E]—dc23   2011048584

The text of this book is set in Futura.
The illustrations are hand-built three-dimensional sets shot
with a Canon digital SLR camera grafted onto the back of a Horseman 4x5 camera.
The line art was drawn with graphite on paper.

MANUFACTURED IN CHINA
10 9 8 7 6 5 4 3 2 1

First Edition

Random House Children's Books supports the First Amendment
and celebrates the right to read.